JOHNNY PENGUIN

by
Dorothy and Marguerite Bryan

Junior Books

DOUBLEDAY, DORAN & COMPANY, INC.

GARDEN CITY · 1941 · NEW YORK

JOHNNY PENGUIN

ONE cold but shining morning, down near the South Pole, Johnny Penguin dozed peacefully and with dignity.

After several shrill calls from Mrs. Penguin, he yawned and stretched.

"Squawk! It is almost time for our chick to eat and there is a big spot on your white waistcoat," said Mrs. Penguin.

"Quawk! All right," said Johnny Penguin amiably.

Johnny was a proud bird with a curly tail. When he had a dirty spot on his vest, be it ever so small, he hurried to wash it off before his neighbors should see it and begin to whisper together about his untidy ways.

The leader penguin came to a crack in the icy snow. He crouched, straightened, crouched . . . leaped across and went on. The second penguin did the same. And the third penguin did the same.

The fourth penguin stopped to look back with pride at the great gap he had jumped. Every penguin following him looked back to see the great gap he had jumped.

Last came Johnny Penguin. He was not content with jumping the same distance as the penguins before him. He sidled along the crack in the ice until he found a much wider gap.

He bobbed down and up three times and hopped high and far across the crack, squawking to attract attention. Out of the corner of his eye he made sure that some of the other penguins had seen him. He looked back with pride at the great gap HE had jumped. And then he waddled on.

They marched on and on and on, over the sparkling snow. Each penguin tried to put his feet in the footprints of the penguin ahead. The untidy penguins going toward the water met another group

of neat, spotless penguins filing back from their swim. They all
stopped. The leaders bowed with much ceremony. Penguins are polite
birds.

Then they all broke ranks and moved about, greeting each other
with deep bows and chatting over penguin affairs.

Johnny told one of the clean penguins about the great jump he
had made. The other penguin could not believe it. Johnny insisted.

Still the other penguin did not believe it. They looked one another up and down coldly—first out of the right eye, then out of the left. Then they held their heads high and squinted along their beaks. And then they fell upon one another, slashing with their beaks and slapping with their flipper-wings.

But the fight was soon over. The clean penguins were terribly upset and Johnny wanted to know why. So he made friends again with the other penguin and asked him about the excitement.

The clean penguins had seen a sea-leopard while in swimming! Their deadliest enemy!! They all croaked about it at once.

At last they separated. The file of clean penguins marched toward the rookery. Johnny and his friends moved on toward the sea. A few of the clean penguins could not resist turning back with them for one more splash. Johnny was in the lead this time.

When they reached the icy ledge that hung over the clear blue water they stood in a row, looking anxiously over the edge with round eyes.

Who should jump first?

Of course, Johnny Penguin strutted forward.

"Who's afraid of sea-leopards?" he asked, and made a beautiful high dive into the water.

All the other penguins dove off after him.

Then the fun began. They looked as though they were flying down there under the water with their short flipper-wings flapping and their little webbed feet trailing out behind to steer by. They popped up high out of the water and plopped back down deep again.

Once when Johnny started up for a breath of air he did not see that a very stout penguin was right above him. Johnny came up hard under this penguin.

"S—Q—U—A—W—K—F!" said the stout penguin. He pretended to be very cross and started to chase Johnny. The other

penguins followed and right away they were playing Follow the Leader.
Johnny tried all sorts of tricks. There were small cakes of ice floating about. He dove under some of these and leaped over others. The penguins dove and leaped after him. He twisted and turned and darted and dashed and popped and plopped. The other penguins followed.

When Johnny Penguin was too tired to play any more he jumped up on a large, flat cake of ice to rest. The other penguins jumped up with him.

Since this ice cake was floating out toward the open sea, they all decided to take a penguin "joy ride."

So they bobbed along happily, standing close together, chattering and squawking greetings to passing penguins.

When Johnny decided that their ice cake had floated out far enough, they all dove off and swam way back and found another flat ice cake. They hopped up on this and rode out again toward the open sea.

Other penguins came, too, until the ice cake was so crowded that the new penguins jumping on pushed the old passengers off the other side. They didn't mind, though. They just caught another excursion ice cake.

Johnny and his friends decided to have "just one more ride" for the fifth or sixth or seventh or eighth time.

They were swimming slowly back to find another ice cake when they met——

—a *sea-leopard!!!*

Now a sea-leopard is not a pleasant animal to meet at any time but when he is AFTER YOU he is a most awesome sight!

He has spots—not pretty speckly-spots but big blobby spots. He has an enormous round head and huge round eyes and bristling whiskers. But most of all, when he is AFTER YOU he has TEETH!!!

So you can imagine that when that big, ugly sea-leopard stuck his head up out of the water Johnny and his friends

S -- C -- A -- T -- T -- E -- R -- E -- D!

The sea-leopard picked Johnny to chase. He could swim ever so much faster than Johnny but he could not turn as quickly, so that clever little penguin did not go in a straight line. He darted and twisted and dodged and swam round and round in curves.

Once when the sea-leopard ALMOST caught him by the tail Johnny sprang far over an ice cake. The big beast had to go deep down under, so he fell behind.

TRAIL OF THE SEA-LEOPARD ○○○○○
JOHNNY PENGUIN'S TRAIL ○○○○○○○

MAP OF THE CHASE

But Johnny's breath was almost gone. He swam more and more slowly.

Poor Johnny raised his head out of the water to look for the shore. It was not very far away now but all along here was a high, icy ledge. Could he jump way up there, out of reach of the sea-leopard, when he was so tired? How he wished he could fly!

Johnny picked his landing spot. He felt as though he might just as well try to jump to one of the clouds far up in the blue sky. But Johnny was a brave bird.

He dove down deep, then he shot up, UP, UP through the water, through the air, and landed PLUNK with both feet exactly where he wanted to land.

Johnny turned and peered over at the cross sea-leopard, rearing

his ugly head out of the water far below.
"You go home," said Johnny Penguin.

Johnny jumped for joy and flapped his flipper-wings.

"It must be *almost* time for the baby to eat" he thought. A penguin is a casual bird.

Johnny scurried along the shore until he found a likely spot.

He dove under the water and gathered a beakful of shrimps.

He tucked these far back in his gullet and waddled quickly toward home.

"I think I'll hurry along," Johnny said to himself.

He got down on his stomach and slid himself over the snow with strong strokes of his flippers and pushes with his feet. He could move much faster that way.

He coasted down the slippery slope of one hill and

paddled hard up to the top of the next.

At last Johnny reached the rookery.

Mrs. Penguin took the shrimps from him and fed them to the hungry penguin chick.

Johnny Penguin dozed peacefully and with dignity, that cold and shining afternoon down near the South Pole.